Chapter 1

Five Crows

"Why would anyone want a crow?" Melvin asked me. "Crows are stupid."

"No they aren't!" I protested, crossing my arms. "Crows are brilliant!"

"I'd rather have a scarecrow for a pet than a crow," Tabitha added. Everyone laughed. At me.

"You know, *someday* you'll appreciate animals for

who they are," I told them. "Mom will never say *no* to getting a crow. I'll even ask her today!"

"Pft!" Melvin scoffed, skeptically. "I bet you'll have *five crows* tomorrow." He was really good at being sarcastic!

"You know what, I've had it!" I shouted. "If I get one crow on Friday morning, you will owe me...20 bucks."

"Deal!" he replied. "Get ready to pay up. I want a new basketball."

"And *I* want five crows," I answered, walking to the swings. *YES!* That was a good comeback.

I hopped on the swing next to Dana and smiled. "I'm getting a crow."

"What?" she asked. "You're mom is *never* going to let you get a *crow*."

"Well, with a little trickering she will," I explained. "I have a plan…"

3 Ways to get your parents to get you a pet

By: Hannah & Kira
Thompson

Do you want to get a
Hamster? A kitten? A dog? A
parakeet? Well, here are three
ways to persuade your
mother and father to buy you
one.

1.   You can offer to buy
    the pet yourself, and take
    care of it yourself. This
    step doesn't usually work,
    but you can try it
    yourself.

2.   You can say you'll do
    anything for it, and then

you end up doing chores for the whole year for no money. Laundry, dishes, sweeping. Most people dislike this decision.

3.   In our opinions, we think this is the best way to get a pet. You bribe. Flowers, cupcakes, washing the dishes. When you tell them you want the animal and then do the bribes, it will definitely most *positively* work. Warning: do not

beg. It will not work if you'd beg.

Thank you for reading this website, we hope you guys use these steps.

COMMENTS

Dog+cat=cute

Thank you for the...um, suggestions. Just saying, you got me grounded. Thanks a lot!

No Love,

Jessica.

Surferdudeforever

Hey, dude, your thing really worked! Thanks for the

crocodile, bro! ~~You people~~
You're the best!

Goofygoofgoof

My parakeet, Cracker, is the best! THANK YOU!!! Ha ha ha ha!

"Yeah, that's not gonna work," I muttered to myself. I shut off the computer and thought. Remember when I told Dana I had a plan? I lied. I didn't have a plan. So I looked up this website on the computer when I got home, and I still didn't have a plan.

"Honey?" Mom asked

me. "Is something up?" She noticed my frustrated face. I smiled.

"Yeah, everything's fine," I answered. As she was about to enter the hall, I stopped her. "Wait!"

"Yes, hun?" she replied. "What's up?"

My voice went up high. "Can I get… a… *crow*?" I twiddled my thumbs and looked down at my shoes. "I'll take care of it and everything, I'll even to chores for the rest of the year for no money!"

"Gale, sweetie, a crow would be… just… too much work!" Mom explained. "If we even got a crow, which we aren't, we couldn't let it inside!" She combed her fingernails through my hair. I shrugged her off. "Now I'll have to give up $20.00!"

"Twenty dollars?" she asked. "Why do you have to give up twenty dollars? Plus, where are you going to get the money?"

"Umm...you?" I answered.

"Umm...no?" she confirmed.

"THAT'S the point, I need the crow so I won't pay twenty dollars!" I explained. "Duh!"

"But when we *get* the crow we'll pay MORE than twenty dollars!" Mom told me. "And don't say 'duh' to me, it's rude, young lady."

"Wait, so we're getting the crow?" I asked. "YES!" She knew I was just joking. I would never get that crow, and the woman had a point! I would spend more money getting the crow than not getting the crow. Unless…

"Hey, Ed!" I exclaimed. "Can I do anything for you?"

"Oh, um, my windows are pretty rusty, thank you," he answered. "And my carpets are covered with cracker crumbs."

"Okay, sure!" I replied. "May I come in?"

"Oh, yes!" Ed said. "You can start downstairs."

I went inside and my eyes widened. "Oh...my...nose-hairs!"

His place was covered, I mean COVERED with windows and carpets that were covered with junk! Yeah, just my luck. So I just started working, one carpet to the next. One window to the next. Sigh. This was going to be a *looooong* ~~day~~ evening.

"DONE!" I finally sighed. The place was

gorgeous! I was so proud of myself. "Ed! I'm finished!"

"Okay, I'll be right down!" he called from upstairs. I heard stomping. I heard gasping. I saw gaping. I saw a smile.

"Oh, god!" he shouted. "I need to get thirty more bucks!" Ed stomped upstairs and stomped down stairs. I saw a crisp fifty dollar bill in his hand! Oh, my gosh! He was going to pay me fifty dollars!

"Here, hold this," he

ordered, giving me the bill. I put it in my pocket thinking he'd take a picture as he reached in his. He pulled out a twenty dollar bill and gave it to me.

"70 dollars?" I asked. "Thank you!"

"What? No!" Ed answered. "Can you please give me back the fifty?"

"Okay…" I said, pulling out the fifty dollars. I gave it to him and he waved goodbye, shutting the door on me. "Bye."

I stomped my foot. "Only twenty dollars for *that*?" I asked myself. "That was the hardest I've ever worked in my life!"

I stomped home and when I went inside, I saw Mom at the dinner table, waiting for me.

"Come on, your dinner's getting cold!" she shouted. "Come eat your noodles!"

I ran over to her and whipped out my twenty dollars. I smacked the bill on the table.

"Twenty...juicy...bucks."

"Is that for paying *Melvin* because you're *not* getting that crow?" Mom asked, chewing on a meatball.

"Mom, it's not for-- wait, how do you know that *Melvin* asked me that?" I inquired.

"Emails," she explained.

"Mom, I **_REALLY_** want a crow!" I begged. "Can we get a crow?"

"You already know the answer, sweetie," she

answered. "We can't get a crow."

"But Mom!" I replied. "Look, it's not just for the scam."

"I know, you really want a crow," Mom said.

"No, that's not all," I exclaimed, drumming on the table. *Tap, tap, tap, tap, tap...tap, tap!* "Look, I know I haven't told you this before...I don't really have a friend. Nobody plays with me. They only tease me and annoy me, and I don't know why." Mom was really listening.

"A bird would be a perfect best friend, but not just any bird," I continued. "A reliable, understanding, smart, crow."

"Aw, you poor thing," she comforted, patting my shoulder. "Well...I guess because it's just you and me...we're getting a crow tomorrow."

"Really?!" I asked. "YES, YES, YES!"

"Under one condition," she added. "Keep him *outside*, you hear me? OUTSIDE."

"Deal!" I exclaimed, shaking her hand. I couldn't believe I was getting a real live crow!!! YAY!!!

Chapter 2

The Accident

Julie bumps into you. What is the right thing to say?

- "Hey, watch where you're going, you!"
- "Oh, I'm sorry!"

I raised my hand.

"Yes, Gale?" Mrs. Pam asked.

"The right answer is *Oh, I'm Sorry!*," I answered. "It's the nicest choice."

"Correct!" she exclaimed. "You should say, *Oh, I'm sorry!* to Julia."

Mrs. Pam erased the whiteboard and started writing another question from her teacher-guide book.

"Hey, Gale, how are you doing on the crow?" Melvin whispered to me. He snickered. "I bet you have five crows already."

"No, I'm getting one today!" I whispered back, proudly.

He scoffed. "Yeah, right."

"Yes, right!" I said.

"Gale, quiet down, don't brag about your right answer," Mrs. Pam ordered.

"But I wasn't-- " I said.

"-- Oh, Gale, be honest," she interrupted. "Now who can answer this question?"

My face turned red. I was mad and embarrassed. I felt like I would cry, but I wasn't actually sad. Sometimes I do that when I'm embarrased. I suck it up.

Recess came quickly since we did a fun activity for

math. We counted by ones, twos, threes, fours, fives, sixes, sevens, eights, and nines in multiplication. It was really funny watching Kevin say seven times eight was 51.

"Hey, Gale, how did you get your Mom to say yes? Did you buy her a thousand diamonds?" Melvin teased.

"She just said...*yes*," I answered.

"You have a terrible poker face," he told me. "I don't believe you."

"Trust me, I *am* getting a crow!" I shouted. "Honest!"

"Prove it. Bring the crow to school on Friday," he replied. "If you don't, you owe me twenty dollars."

"Melvin, no pets in school!" I told him. "That's not fair!"

"Maybe no pets *in* school, but what about recess?" he asked. He left with suspicion rising in the air.

I sighed. How could I get a crow and bring it to school? And suddenly an idea sprung at me. What if the crow was the class pet? I'd have to ask Mrs. Pam the next day, but first, I'd have to get the crow.

"Mom, when are we going to get the crow?" I asked Mom when I got home from school. I looked in the kitchen and she had her black raincoat on and her purse in her hand. "We have to go."

"Wait, are we going to be back soon?" I asked. "I want to go get the crow soon."

"Honey, we can't get the crow today," she answered. "Your aunt got hurt."

"What?" I said. "What happened? Which Aunt?"

"Save the questions for after," she replied. "We need to go."

I was so confused. I was so scared. What had happened? I was disappointed. I felt like I was going to cry. Was there an accident?

Soon we were at the hospital. There was a lady

with short, red hair and blue eyes behind the front counter. She smiled at us. "How can I help you?"

"We're visiting Gretchen Solomon," Mom answered. "My name is Dana Kettle."

"Okey, dokey," the lady replied. "Room 58."

I followed Mom upstairs to room 58 and saw Aunt Gretchen. She was in two casts: one on her leg and the other around her neck.

"What happened?" I asked.

"Your Aunt Gretchen was in a car accident," Mom explained. "That's why we didn't buy your crow today."

The door opened behind me. Uncle Don walked in with a meal on a tray. It had two chicken wings, carrots, apples, and a water.

"Here you go, my beloved," he said to Gretchen. "Some wings, veggies, and water."

"Thank you," she answered. Her voice was scratchy. I couldn't believe I couldn't get the crow. At least it was only Tuesday, I had two more days to get the animal. I mean... I also love Aunt Gretchen and I'm worried about her…

We were at the hospital until 7:00 P.M. and we got home at 7:47. I was out like a light at 8:00, and I dreamed about giving Melvin $20.00 in shame, everyone looking at me. I didn't want that to really happen.

Beep! Beep! Beep! my alarm repeated. I rolled over

on my side and hit the *snooze* button. I rolled back over when Mom walked in and picked me up out of bed. She carried me down the staircase and plopped me on the couch with a *Ugh!*

"Would you like some oatmeal, darling?" she asked me, walking into the kitchen. She sounded like she was in a good mood.

"Yes, please, darling!" I exclaimed. I giggled. "Oatmeal would be magnificent!"

"Magnificent, what a magnificent word!" she answered.

So I ate my oatmeal and got ready for school and all of that stuff, and then I headed off to the building of education.

What is the right thing to say when someone is talking when they're not supposed to?

- "SHUSH, YOU'RE GOING TO GET IN TROUBLE!!!"

- "Umm, can you please quiet down?"
- Not say anything, tap their shoulder, and place your finger in the middle of your lips vertically.

"Can anyone answer this question?" Mrs. Pam asked the class when school started. "Melvin?"

Four people raised their hands: Me, Melvin, Nona, and Reese.

"The first option: *SHUSH! YOU'RE GOING*

TO GET IN TROUBLE!'" Melvin answered. He laughed, and everyone else did, too. Except for Nona and me.

"Now, Melvin, we won't have any monkey business in here, got it?" Mrs. Pam announced. "That's a warning, Mr."

"Got it," Melvin replied, laughing hysterically. Callie was laughing so hard her face looked like a tomato that was turning purple.

Nona and I kept raising our hands. Reese put his hand down. I guess he was going to say the same thing as Melvin. Just to be funny.

"Nona?" Mrs. Pam called. I put my hand down. I knew Nona would answer it correctly.

"The second option: *Umm, could you please quiet down?*" she answered. Hmm, she was wrong and I was wrong because I thought she would get it right!

"I'm sorry, that is incorrect," Mrs. Pam said.

I raised my hand back up and she called on me. "The third option: *Not say anything, tap their shoulder, and place your finger in the middle of your lips vertically.*"

"Correct!" she exclaimed, clapping her hands together twice.

"Smarty pants," Melvin whispered. He was obviously calm now. "Two more days for you, including today…"

He tickled my neck but I nudged it off.
ANNOYING!!!

I had to ask Mrs. Pam for my future crow to be the class pet. Well, I had to get the crow before I asked. So I had to wait until Thursday.

After recess, we went inside and started science class. We were mixing sand, gravel and dirt which Mrs. Airy called *humus*. Suddenly, the fire drill alarm sounded.

"THIS IS NOT A DRILL, REPEAT, NOT A

DRILL!" Principal Pozina shouted on the intercom. "FILE OUTSIDE LIKE USUAL, BUT QUICK!"

We ran outside. What was happening? Was there a real fire? Was our school going to be alright? What if somebody got hurt? These questions went round and round in my head. And what really worried me, was that Mrs. Pam looked worried. She was biting her fingernails and everything. What I mostly didn't want, was for the fire to spread and ruin our school.

Chapter 3

Allison Shaved *Bob* in my Head!

I was so, SO relieved that the fire didn't hurt the school and the fire department got there on time. I told my Mom all about the adventure we had.

"First, we were waiting outside for the fire to go out, when we heard a bark. We turned around and we saw a stray dog! He was a golden retriever and he chased after Mrs. Pam! It was biting air and barking and barking. It ran so fast that it caught on to Mrs. Pam's skirt! There was a huge rip and we could see her underwear! Poor Mrs. Pam. After the dog bit her skirt, he ran away into the woods," I explained. "And she had to get a skirt from the nurse's office! Next, we were standing, and then suddenly, Reese called out, *Grape Berry Candy!* and everyone laughed, including me. And I never laugh at jokes! It really cheered me up from the fire. When I heard the fire was out, I was so happy and relieved and sort of scared. What if it happened again someday? I thought."

"Well, it won't happen again, sweetie," Mom told me. "Now first we're getting you a haircut and then we're getting you a crow."

"Yes!" I exclaimed. "Finally! Can I bring it to school for class pet?"

"Mrs. Pam would never let you bring it to school," she answered. "Honey, that wouldn't work, unless … you had a trained crow."

"Okay, then let's get a trained crow!" I announced, smiling. "At the pet store!"

"Do they have trained crows at the pet store?" Mom asked. "I haven't even seen a *regular* crow at the pet store."

"Well, then...let's check!" I exclaimed. "Let's go!"

"Okay…" she agreed while I pulled her arm out the door. "Wait, I need my coat!"

"Oh, sorry," I blushed. I let her go inside and get her coat and shoes on.

We were in our silver minivan about five minutes later, driving to the barber shop. When we were there, we walked inside and saw that the place was empty! Perfect! We could get this haircut over with and then go get my crow.

"Hello, welcome to Cut's Cuts," a lady in green said right when we entered the shop. "My name is Allison and I will be cutting your hair today."

She walked over to the computer they have behind the counter and clicked a couple buttons and scrolled down a little bit.

"The Kettle's?" she asked, looking up from the monitor.

"Yes," Mom answered. "Gale here is going first."

She gestured to me with her hands. I walked to one of the black chairs and waited for my smock.

"We decided we would like to get a bob for her," Mom explained to Allison. "A short little Bob."

It was funny what she did. Well, funny for my classmates...but **not** me. It was terrible! She literally shaved "BOB" on the top of my head! Mom tried to stop her but it was too late. *That's* why the place was empty.

"WHAT?!" I shrieked. Mom and I left without paying a cent. Mom colored with brown marker on the top of my head, but it didn't make a difference.

After the terrid (terrible/horrid) experience at Cut's Cuts, we went to the pet store. I was *so* angry at that Allison! We would never go to that barber shop again!

Chapter 4

Mom Here

Hi, it's Gale's mom here. Gale has no idea that when we go to the pet store, there will be no crow. And *especially* not a trained crow. She's going to be *so* disappointed when she finds out she has to pay that *Melvin* $20.00. She says everyone will be staring at her and she'll be so embarrassed. I know, as a parent, I should've said right away, "No, we're not getting a crow and that's final!" but when I heard that the crow would be her best friend and all that junk, I felt so bad I just had to try. When she said she wanted to have it as a school pet, I automatically thought, *NO way*. If we were to get a crow, the easiest way to get it would be to shoot one in the wild and carry it home. When we got home from the pet store, Gale was so sad. She faced the truth, that's how it goes.

"Patty, oh, yes, umm...can you and Teresa and Terrence come over to dinner Saturday?" I whispered into the phone. I didn't want Gale to hear.

"OH, that's so nice of you!" she exclaimed. "I would LOVE to!"

"Great," I answered. "See you then, bye!"

"Bye!" she replied.

"Who was that?" I heard a voice say. I turned around

and saw Gale standing there, her cheeks wet. It was 8:04, so she had her pajamas on.

"It was... the oil guy!" I answered. "Yes…"

"So the oil guy's name is Patty and you're inviting him over for dinner on Saturday?" she joked. But it wasn't supposed to be funny. She was crying about the crow, crossing her arms in her footies.

"Okay, fine, I was calling Teresa over and her parents so you can make a friend," I confessed. "Remember when you had a speech about the crow? Well, since you said the crow would be your friend, I'm getting you another friend!"

"What if I don't like her?" she asked. "What if I don't get along with her?"

"Umm, I never thought of that… maybe you'll get another friend at school?" I suggested.

"I already have Dana!" She shouted. "I lied, okay? I do have *one* friend! I just wanted to beat the challenge and honestly...I haven't let go of Bringer."

"Honey, we can't do anything about Bringer," I answered. "We can't take anything back."

"But Mom, we can buy another bird!" She exclaimed, sobbing, her tears getting larger by the millisecond. "It will heal me!" She did that *form-a-tiny-smile-when-you're-crying-but-then-go-back-to-a-crying-frown-right-*

after thing. That *It will heal me!* was definitely dramatic.

"Hun, if we were to get a bird, we would get another parakeet, not a crow!" I answered. "A crow would be crazy! And just to be clear, we're *not*, I mean NOT… getting a parakeet. And twenty dollars wouldn't hurt, right?"

"What if everyone teased me and made fun of me because I was saying how amazing a crow was and then I lost a bet to getting one?"

she asked. "I would be heartbroken if I got teased more than I usually do."

"Gale, a crow is not a pet!" I yelled. "Now go to bed!"

She stomped up to her room while I sighed a big sigh. This was going to be a long day.

Chapter 5
<u>Gale's Back</u>

___Hi, Gale again. It's 6:23, and I have to go to school at seven o'clock. So at 6:30, I'm going to get ready for school. I keep thinking in my head, *BGIF*: Blame God It's Friday. Instead of: *TGIF*: Thank God It's Friday. Melvin's going to attack me with teasing. He's going to push me around. Literally. He pushes me around the playground at recess.

So I got out of bed 7 minutes later to get dressed in jeans and a t shirt with a green thumb on the front of it with the words: *Go Green!* overlapping it. After I did, I brushed my hair and ate some homemade french toast. I brushed my teeth next, and ended the routine with grabbing the twenty dollars. Oh, boy.

Which choice is the right thing to do when your friend is being bullied?

- Stand there and watch he/her be bullied and pushed around.
- Stand up for them and stop the bully.
- Beat up the bully and gain punishment.

My friends choose the first choice. After Joshua answered that question, it was math time, and after math time was recess. I swang on the swings for two minutes and then said goodbye to Dana. I was going to give the cash to my enemy.

"Here's the money, Melvin," I said to him. He was leaning against a tree, his cheeks wet. "We all know, I lose, I'm the loser." I handed him the twenty dollar bill, but he didn't take it.

"No, keep it," he answered, his voice trembling. "I don't deserve it."

"Melvin, what's wrong?" I asked. "What happened?"

"My family had to put my dog down," he explained. "It was last night…"

"Aw, I'm sorry," I answered sympathetically. "I lost Bringer the bird, I know how you feel."

"A dog is more than a stupid bird!" Melvin shouted.

I wasn't mad. When I get sad, I get angry, too. Like when I stomped up to my room because I couldn't get the crow.

"I know," I muttered.

"I'm sorry the way I treated you," he apologized. "It was wrong. Mom told me to say that, but I really mean it."

"Thank you," I thanked. "Friends?"

"Yeah, I guess," he answered, smiling. He wiped off his tears and we fistbumped. He swung with me and Dana. "Crow's aren't stupid." … I guess we lived happily ever after… until that afternoon…

"And then we lived happily ever after," I told Mom. On the TV, something caught my attention. It was about crows.

"People have been shooting crows, and earth has been losing more and more by day and night!" an old lady explained to the newscaster. "It's terrible! My scarecrow business has gone down a lot!"

"INteresting…" The newscaster replied. "How do

you know this information, ma'am?"

"First of all, it's young lady, second, I hear gunshots at night. My cat gets scared and she told me that she wanted to move out of Florida and go somewhere else," she answered.

"Um, young lady, your cat talks to you?" the newscaster asked. He looked at her firmly.

"Yes," she told him, facing the camera.

"Losing crows?" I asked Mom.

"That's what I heard," she told me. "There *are* crows in Florida, and old people that talk to cats."

"We *have* to help them!" I exclaimed. "Can we go to Florida?"

"Honey, we don't have the money!" she answered. I couldn't help laughing. That rhymed.

I snapped into serious mode. "Mom, it's April

vacation! Would it help if I gave you my twenty dollars?"

"Keep that," she told me.

"Okay, good, I totally wanted to keep it," I confessed. "I'll call Melvin and tell him about the crow incident in Florida."

679-342-85 was his number and after I dialed that in the phone, he answered.

"Hello?" he asked. "Melvin Victors here!"

"Yes, it's Gale Kettle," I answered. "I got to tell you something."

"Proceed," he replied.

"The earth is losing crows because hunters are shooting them in Florida!" I explained. "Mom won't take me there!"

"Still into crows, eh, Gale?" Melvin asked. "Well, on April Vacation (tomorrow), we're going to Florida! Maybe I could help with that!"

"Oh my, gosh," I answered. "Thank you so much, Melvin, it's great thinking a friend can handle

this kind of thing. Bye!" I
hung up the phone.

"What did he say?" Mom
asked. I told her what he said
and she smiled. "Great!
That's amazing!"

Chapter 6

We're Going to Jacksonville!

Hi, it's Melvin here. And I'm going to Florida in an hour and helping Gale. Some people like Gale's mom might think I'm a fake and I'm not her friend, but I like Gale. She *is* my friend. When I was mean, my dog was already sick and it just made me sad and when I'm sad I'm mad. When she died, I was really sad. So I yelled at Gale, and she understood. That's a real friend right there.

We got in the car at 12:00. By *we* I mean: my two brothers, Juan the adopted one and Mark my actual brother, my big sister, Courtney, Mom and Dad. And no dog.

Courtney, Mom and Dad sang "The wheels on the car go round and round, round and round, round and round, the wheels on the car go round and round, until we get to the airport!" It was really annoying. I think they did it purposely to annoy us.

When we got to the airport, we weighed our bags and all of that stuff. Then we went to Shirley's and got to eat pizza. Of course, I only got cheese. Mom knows how I *hate* pepperoni. After we waited in line for a black to-go box and a meal, we went to gate C4. We got on the plane after I played *KILL* for about a half an hour. I was in the window seat, Juan was in the middle, and Mark was in the aisle seat.

"Dude, are you watching *Grant Chicken* playing Kill?" I asked Juan. "That guy stinks at that game!"

"Really?" he asked. "I think he's pretty good, he's letting the zombies eat him."

Mark slapped himself in the forehead with his hand. I did that, too.

"No, you have to be bad to be good at the game," he explained. "If you let yourself die, you're bad at the game."

"Oh, so the objective of the game is to be bad and kill stuff," Juan realized in his accent. "*That's* why it's called Kill!"

We taught him how to play and Mark beat both of us. He *is* the oldest. I mean, 9, 10, 11 (I'm ten by the way).

We were in Florida at 5:00, so we were going out for dinner. We went to this

Restaurant called Tim and Lee's and I got the chicken fingers and home fries. I got soda and sliced banana, too. After that, we walked by the water and then on the way back we bought ice cream. I got Death By Chocolate. It's called that because it tastes like heaven.

The next day, mission one started: go to the sheriff's office and tell him to report all hunters to his office.

"Mom, can I go to the sheriff's office?" I asked

Mom that day. "I'm groomed, dressed, and ready!"

"Melvin, why do you need to go to the sheriff's office?" she asked me. "Oh, is this about the *crow incident* you were talking about yesterday?"

"Yes," I answered. "Can I?"

"If I come with you," she replied.

"Okay, I was going for tough, but as long as I can go, I'm okay with bringing my

Mom," I explained. "Now vaminos!"

When we were at the sheriff's office, I was surprised. I thought it would be a man, but a woman was sitting in the big black chair with the big black dog sitting next to her. The word *Madison* was on her nametag.

"How can I help you?" she asked in her southern accent.

"Um, I'll explain if you call down all of the hunters to this here office," I answered.

"Don't worry, we're not going to hurt you."

"First I need a reason, young man," Madison told me in a tough voice.

"I wanted to give a speech to them about the earth losing crows because they're hunting them," I explained. "For my friend."

"Alright," she agreed, grabbing a walkie talkie out of her pocket. She pressed a button and held it until she was done talking. "All hunters come down to the sheriff's office immediately."

Two minutes later hunters started coming inside.

"What is it?" one growled. "There was a crow flying by and you made me miss it!"

"Actually, this speech is about crows," I told him.

"Stay out of this, kid," he scowled.

"He's the one that called you down here," Madison explained. "He's the head of this operation."

"In that case, why'd you bring us down here, kid?" he asked me.

"I'll tell you when everyone's here," I said.

"I'm the only hunter in Florida that hunts crows, little man," he told me. "What do you have to say?"

"*You're* the only one?" I repeated, surprised. "Okey, dokey…" I pulled out my flash cards. I wrote this on them:

It's important to have crows. Why? Here are some

examples: What about halloween? ~~All of y~~You, hunter,~~s~~ ~~are~~ you're amazing, but hunting is actually very bad. We need animals on earth. Killing a bird is mean and evil. What if someone shot you and you died and they ate you? They're very important. Especially a crow. Crows are important on earth. Please stop hunting them. Here are some other reasons that crows are important: They are very smart animals, and we might need them on earth. They have excellent memory. Please stop hunting them. By: MELVIN.

I presented this speech to the hunter but it didn't change anything.

"So you're pretty much saying crows are useless," He answered. "Yeah, I'll keep hunting them. Thanks."

"You know he worked hard on that speech," the sheriff said making the hunter stop and turn around. "You could at least give him something."

"Okay," he agreed.

"Good speech kid. Now bye."

The sheriff let him leave after that. "Kid, we gotta talk. Sit down in the chair."

"Yeah?" I answered. "What is it?"

"Did you come here just for the crows?" Madison wondered. She put her hand on my shoulder. "Sun, there are a lot of crows in the world. Just because one hunter is shooting them in Florida doesn't mean all of them are going to be gone.

Remember when you said they were smart? They're so smart that they can find ways to stay alive."

I understood. There are more crows in the world, not just in Florida.

"First, this is my vacation," I told her. "Second, thanks for the talk."

"Anytime, kid," she answered.

I left the sheriff's office and enjoyed my April Vacation.

Chapter 7

Five Crows

Gale here again. Melvin explained that he couldn't stop the hunting and that there are many crows in the world. I'm grateful I have what I have, I don't need a crow. Maybe it's my dream, but I don't need five crows. At least not yet.

This book was written and designed by Claire Burbank
Typeset in IM Fell English

66740154R00050

Made in the USA
Middletown, DE
14 March 2018